The Pilfered Quill

Rachel Rener & David Green

© 2024 Lightning Conjurer Books, LLC

All rights reserved. No portion of this book may be reproduced in any form without permission from the author, except for the use of brief quotations in a book review.

This is a work of fiction. Names, characters, businesses, places, events, locales, and incidents are either the products of the author's imagination or used in a fictitious manner. Any resemblance to actual persons, living or dead, or actual events is purely coincidental.

Edited by Sarah Chorn

Cover by Miblart

ASIN: B0CMT3T1ZS
ISBN: 9798866081332

*For all the writers whose literary genius was
never properly appreciated.*

VIVALDI'S '*CONCERTO IN F MINOR*' pulled Chet Williams from the recurring nightmare that had been plaguing him for more than a decade: a triumphant vision of him striding up to the podium to accept his Nobel Prize in Literature, only to realize he wasn't wearing pants, and the name they had called was not 'Chet Williams,' but 'Jon A. Williams' – the nom de plume of his far more successful younger brother.

Chet flipped onto his back with a groan and let his head sink into his pillow, allowing Vivaldi's lilting violins to banish the clinging thoughts of his brother, the multi-million-book selling, award-winning, critically acclaimed fantasy author extraordinaire. But not even the Italian maestro's greatest masterpiece could free Chet from the grip of Jon's accomplishments, manifold, wide-ranging, and insufferable as they were. Not only had his younger sibling of *exactly* two years – fate had landed an early insult by giving them both the same birthday – landed an agent with the very first manuscript he'd ever written, but Jon stood six inches taller, had always attracted more attention from the opposite sex, and possessed a blemish free, symmetrical face with healthy sinuses. Adding insult to injury, *no one* – not their parents, not their extended family, not Jon's agents or legions of fans – seemed to notice what an ignorant, arrogant hack the man was.

No one!

A sharp pain zinged through Chet's jaw.

"Stop grinding your teeth!" he groaned, rubbing at his chin as his meticulously chosen alarm tone strove to spirit him away to a higher realm of creativity and beauty. His favorite author, G.R.R. Kingfisher, had once said in an interview that he always woke to Vivaldi. Always. And if it was good enough for G.R.R...

Chet scowled, the ache in his jaw refusing to subside. He'd forgotten to wear his mouth guard again. Something Jon would *never* have to shove into his perfect mouth of sparkling white teeth.

It's his fault I started grinding my teeth in the first place! he fumed. After his brother's third Hugo Award, Chet had written him a lengthy missive filled with obligatory praise on Jon's latest "success" – a steaming mound of trite, platitudinous garbage, to be sure. Chet hadn't bothered reading it. After heaping on the socially acceptable amount of curried favor, Chet suggested Jon forward the attached manuscript – Chet's latest – to his agent and possibly, *possibly*, make an introduction. And while he was at it, a meet-and-greet with Jon's renowned editor wouldn't go amiss either. Chet had sacrificed so much for his younger brother over the years, after all – the sanctimony of his birthday, for one. The top bunk in their room. He had even let his little brother use the funky GameCube controller when they played Mario

Kart Double Dash as kids. Really, this one *tiny* favor was the least Jon could do.

But no.

Much to Chet's chagrin, Jon's reply had been anything but civil. Or gracious. One might say it was downright hostile, smug, and oh-so-superior – much like everything else that came out of his little brother's smirking mouth.

"Telling me I have to earn an agent like he did." Chet wiped away the angry tears stinging his eyes. "Like *he* worked for *anything*! I came up with Geran's name in his first book! The most important aspect. Jon was going to call him Gerat. *Gerat*! And did he give me credit? No! Just a measly acknowledgement in the back to his 'big brother'. He didn't even write *Chet*!"

With the blissful string melody still emanating from his cellphone, Chet huffed himself into a sitting position, propped up by his compressed pillow, and glared around his one-room, Tallahassee apartment. Daylight filtered in through the ratty curtains, heating his room like an oven before the day even started, while shining a harsh light on his depressed two-seater sofa, modest TV, and cramped kitchen space.

Chet ignored it all, his eyes falling on his beloved workstation, his pride and joy. The stand-by light on his computer monitor faded and pulsed a calming blue. He stared at it, his fingers clutching and letting go of the bed cover in time.

Squeezing his eyes shut, Chet breathed in and out, centering himself to Vivaldi, just like G.R.R. Kingfisher did. *He'd* faced plenty of rejection before his most recent series had changed the face of urban fantasy forever. *He* hadn't let criticisms of his supposed "misogynistic and basic" style get the better of him. *He* persevered, despite the flood of one-star reviews that plagued his early books – the result of woke cancel culture that couldn't handle the overwhelming enormity of his talent. His *vision*. If G.R.R. Kingfisher could endure all of that and come out on the other side a shining exemplar of success, well…

A slow smile broke out across Chet's face, the lilting calm of Vivaldi finally transporting him to that higher mental plane he was constantly seeking to attain. Doubt didn't exist there. Neither did anger.

Nor did Jon.

Chet flicked off his alarm and eyed the pulsing blue glow of his monitor. Words would be written today. Many words. Fantastic words. Possibly some not-so-great words, but they would be vastly overshadowed by the aforementioned fantastic words.

"First, coffee." Chet pulled his covers clear and swung his legs out of bed. "Genius can never be attained without coffee. I'm sure that's the same for Vivaldi *and* G.R.R. Kingfisher."

Chet's cellphone rattled with furious urgency, vying for his attention from atop his cluttered nightstand. He snatched it up. Upon seeing the notification waiting for him, his stomach lurched like a rowboat traversing the Atlantic in mid-winter.

A response from Maddcraft Publishing about a query he'd sent three months ago stared him in the eye. His mouth went dry. Their website mentioned a six-month wait for self-represented manuscripts. He'd name-dropped Jon in his cover letter of course, which might have gotten him bumped up the line, but a response already? From Maddcraft?

His fingers itched. They demanded to swipe the notification and his eyes begged to devour the news, but Chet set the phone down gently. Reverently. Such portentous news couldn't be read on a mere five-and-a-half-inch screen; they required his 4k super-wide monitor! Happy news such as this—and it *would* be happy, he knew it—needed to be consumed in the same place the magic was made.

Working to steady his thumping heart and twisting guts, Chet crossed to his cramped kitchen and flicked on the kettle. Coffee would accompany him on his quest to read Maddcraft's missive. Then, after graciously accepting their desire to publish his work, he'd send a casual message to his parents. He'd let *them* inform Jon. When his baby brother came crawling back to share some of his elder's success, Chet would pass it off as no big deal, knowing Jon would vociferously assure him that it *was*. Maddcraft wasn't one of the 'Big Five' publishing houses, but they were widely acclaimed and highly rated on Yelp. *And* Chet had secured their favor – and their forthcoming contract – *without* an agent or his brother's overrated editor.

"I didn't even use an editor." Chet smiled, pouring piping hot water into his mug. "Never have and never will. I'm sure Maddcraft will agree there's no point in tampering with perfection."

Taking a gulp of steaming black gold, Chet settled in front of his monitor, hand hovering over the mouse, fingers trembling. Forcing a volley of quick breaths from his lungs, he clicked, the butterflies in his stomach swirling like a tempest as the computer hummed to life. After refreshing his email inbox, he positioned the cursor over Maddcraft's reply, then, with a nod, pressed on it.

Dear C.R.R.T. Williams, the letter began. Chet momentarily lingered on his pen name, which still didn't sound grand enough. Maybe another letter needed adding. Perhaps a 'J'? They always looked good.

"Dear C.R.R.T. Williams," he continued, reading the letter aloud to himself, "we thank you so much for your query. Let us assure you, we here at Maddcraft Publishing are well-aware of, and are big admirers of, your brother, Jon A.

Williams." Chet scowled. Just because *he* had mentioned Jon didn't mean everyone else had to. Clearing his throat, he continued on. "Your manuscript, '*The Magician's Apprentice's Daughter*' has some promise for a first draft." Chet leaned back in his chair, grinning. *Promise!* "However, there are some issues." Chet's grin abruptly evaporated. His reading grew hastier and more mumbled as he skimmed the remainder of the letter.

"Firstly, the submission window was for full-length epic fantasy novels. A novel in this genre is generally around one-hundred-and-twenty-thousand words, minimum. '*The Magician's Apprentice's Daughter*' is barely thirty-thousand words, and five-thousand of those comprise a glossary of characters and terms. Secondly, there are some dubious depictions of women included, especially the eponymous warlock's apprentice's daughter, who doesn't actually have a name. Was this an oversight or a choice? Either way, this speaks to the problematic usage of anyone who isn't male in your novelette."

Chet sipped at his coffee, eyes narrowing

even further.

"Thirdly, the manuscript, even for a first draft, is littered with spelling mistakes and poor usage of grammar and punctuation. Not only that, but there are at least three major plot holes, two unresolved story arcs, and the ending is confusing. Why did the magician's apprentice's daughter decide to give her power and inheritance to Chête? More troubling, the manuscript is called *'The Magician's Apprentice's Daughter'* but the male character reaps all the reward and praise once the quest is completed, and the daughter is treated like an afterthought. She's barely in the final two chapters, unless you count her silently standing in the background. Sadly, with all this in mind, we will not be taking your submission further. It is only because of our great admiration for your younger brother that we responded, with the strong recommendation that you hire a developmental editor. Even better, your brother might be kind enough to give you some pointers. Yours, The Maddcraft Team."

Chet's mouse crashed into the opposite wall, sending shards of broken plastic ricocheting across the room.

"How dare they?!" he howled, tears streaming down his reddened cheeks. "My *brother?!* I wouldn't let that hack read my work even if he begged me!"

He grabbed the monitor, his fingernails digging into the plastic as he shook it, throttling it like it was the entire Maddcraft editorial team. "Damn you, Maddcraft!" he raged, spraying the screen with spittle and ire. "You'll never have my work! You'll be sorry, just like the rest of them!"

The monitor rattled and flickered in a resigned manner. For the 4k, super-wide display word processor, it was just another Saturday morning under the stewardship of C.R.R.T. Williams.

He let go of his monitor and sank back into his chair, his bottom lip thrust out and trembling. "They don't get it, is all. Maddcraft just doesn't get what I'm trying to do… Idiots! Just like the rest of them!"

Sniffing, he opened a new browser, using the keyboard to do so. He'd had plenty of practice. The slain mouse was but one of many.

Chet typed in G.R.R. Kingfisher's website's address. Reading about his hero's many rejections always made him feel better. It had been two weeks since the last affront of Chet's genius, and G.R.R. always updated his blog with jocular stories and slices of life.

When Chet saw the most recent blog update, his jaw dropped open and his hand jerked forward, knocking his mug of coffee to the floor.

G.R.R. Kingfisher was dead.

"No," Chet whispered, wiping at his eyes, his blood going from hot to cold in the space of the website's loading time. "No! No, no, *nooo!*" he wailed, shaking his hands at the sky. "Not G.R.R.!"

Chet had moved to Tallahassee because G.R.R. Kingfisher lived there. He listened to Vivaldi, drank his coffee strong and black, and added extra letters to his name because G.R.R. Kingfisher had. Chet had kept writing despite his numerous rejections because G.R.R. Kingfisher had.

And now he was dead.

Chet skimmed through obituaries of the

deceased author, too stunned to produce tears. It happened a week ago. They'd already buried him. A shock, many said. He had no family to speak of and hadn't left a will as he'd passed relatively young and unexpectedly. Chet paused on that nugget as he leaned forward.

Lawyers were holding an estate sale at G.R.R. Kingfisher's place, starting an hour from now. Chet launched to his feet, leaving his monitor on, and threw on the previous day's rumpled clothes.

An estate sale at G.R.R. Kingfisher's. Chet had to go. He *had* to. Only fate knew what he might find there—what slice of inspiration— and he wouldn't let anything of worth fall into another's grubby hands.

Scooping up his cellphone, Chet slammed his apartment door behind him, leaving the mouse's innards, shards of porcelain, and once-warm coffee splattered across the floor.

Two

With engine protesting and tires squealing, Chet's 1979 Ford Pinto careened up the two-mile-long driveway that led to G.R.R. Kingfisher's estate, a refurbished plantation tucked among a forest of gnarled Lichgate oaks and Loblolly pines that strategically hid the white monstrosity of a mansion from public view. By the time he slammed the car door behind him – momentarily catching the hem of his tweed jacket until he ripped it free – Chet was panting and sweating as though he'd spent the morning trudging through the swamps that made up the majority of G.R.R. Kingfisher's sprawling estate.

Without sparing a second glance at his lush surroundings, Chet bounded up the driveway, now a makeshift parking lot for the dozens of cars parked there, elbowing and shoving past half-lidded bargain shoppers who haphazardly clutched history itself in their greedy, grubby paws: a stack of leather bound books, framed portraits, a tweed jacket – much like his own – that Chet immediately recognized from the last interview G.R.R. had ever given.

With a strangled cry, he flung himself up the porch stairs and through the propped open double doors, where his eyes bulged at the sight of at least two dozen people casually milling about G.R.R.'s foyer, perusing a long line of tables that had been haphazardly stacked with the late genius' discounted belongings as though they were at some front-yard garage sale.

"How much will you take for this bowl?" an old woman asked one of the tan-suited attendants who was making rounds with a pen and clipboard in hand.

"Hmm…" the man replied, straightening his glasses as he ran a finger down the extensive list. "It looks like the ceramic dishware is going for five dollars apiece."

The woman crinkled her nose, setting the bowl back on the table with a dismissive sniff.

"How dare you!" Chet snarled, snatching the bowl and clutching it against his chest like a newborn babe. "Do you know what this is?" The woman opened her mouth to answer, but Chet barreled on, "This is G.R.R. Kingfisher's bowl! His *bowl!* The very thing from which he spooned cereal and soup and porridge and all sorts of foods that are more liquid than solid, while musing over his next chapter or forthcoming spark of brilliance!" Chet seized the priceless spoon the woman was inspecting. "Give me that, you oblivious shrew!"

"Well I never!" the woman gasped, clutching her pearls.

With the wide-eyed, frenzied countenance of an addict, Chet wove between the throngs of ignorant lummoxes, snatching, pilfering, and filching every item he could, until his arms were too laden to carry even one more fountain pen. After his third trip to his car, which was stuffed so full he couldn't see anything out his rear window, he sank into the driver's seat, panting and heaving. Beside him, boxes and boxes of "junk" were stacked on top of one another – boxes of notebooks, bath towels, Tupperware, tins of paperclips, wax seals, debris from G.R.R.'s office garbage bin, and an assemblage of pens and quills that those imbecilic buffoons had marked at fifty cents apiece.

"Thank God I got here on time," Chet huffed, studying the tiny amount of empty space left in his car and the mansion's propped-open front doors as he quickly calculated how many dollars – or perhaps cents – he still had in his bank account. "Not enough," he groaned, raking his fingers through his hair.

A flutter of movement outside the house made his head jerk up. The tan-suited attendants had ushered everyone out the front doors and were in the process of bolting them shut.

"I didn't even have time to savor being in his home," he croaked. "To walk where he walked, to sit where he sat, to use the toilet where he…" His voice cracked with emotion. "I never got to send him my manuscript," he whispered against his knuckles. "We could have been such good friends, G.R.R. and me."

"G.R.R. and 'I,'" a phantom voice whispered from the passenger seat.

"No, because 'me' is the object, not the—" Chet let out a sharp gasp upon remembering he was the sole occupant of the car. "What the— Who's there?" he demanded, craning his neck to inspect the back seat.

"Not 'who,' but 'what,' as 'who' can only refer to a person, and even then, only if the person is the subject rather than the object."

Chet whirled back around so quickly his neck cracked. "I—*What?!*"

"'Who' should only be used to refer to the subject of a sentence, while 'whom' must be used to refer to the object of a verb or preposition."

"G.R.R, is that…is th-that y-you?" Chet stuttered, his head swiveling as he searched for his ghostly companion. "D-Do you need me to finish the last book in your 'Falston Records' series?" His hopes soared alongside the idea. *G.R.R.'s spirit, come back from the dead to enlist* me *in the completion of his life's greatest work!*

"Ghosts exist but in stories, you lamentable meat puppet! Now let me out of this box!"

"Box…?" Chet snatched the smallest carton from the top of G.R.R.'s teetering pile of reclaimed belongings, frantically rooting around it for the source of the voice. "Where are you?" he demanded shrilly.

"I am on every page of Shakespeare's poetry, Hemingway's prose, and Dylan's lyrics."

"What?!"

"I am Icarus' hubris, Gatsby's greed, and Hamlet's folly. I am as everlasting as time and as ubiquitous as the wind."

A box of cutlery went flying and crashing into the back seat as Chet feverishly began digging around the next box he could get his hands on.

"I am truth. I am travesty. I am terror! My incomparable might far surpasses that of a swo—"

"Aha!" Chet exclaimed in triumph, plucking a lavish black ostrich feather quill from the carton of office supplies he'd pilfered from the roped-off section of G.R.R.'s study.

"*Unhand me, you ham-fisted troglodyte!*" the writing tool barked.

Eyes widening, then narrowing, Chet hunched over the quill, inspecting it. The feather was long and luxurious, albeit worn, and the shaft was encased in an ornately engraved metal tube, which had peculiar shapes and symbols etched along the length of it. It ended with a sharp metal nib which drew blood when Chet pressed his finger against it.

"Ow!" he muttered, sucking on his finger. "You bit me!"

"*If I had my mouth, I would bite; if I had my liberty, I would do my liking!*"

"I-Is…is that Twain?" Chet stammered.

"*It is Shakespeare, you bucktoothed buffoon! And for that matter, not even Shakespeare is Shakespeare! I am Shakespeare, just as I am Homer, Orwell, Hemingway, Dickinson, Vonnegut, Kingfisher, and—*"

"What did you just say?" Chet's jaw dangled open and closed. "D-Did you just say K-Kingf-fisher? As in, *G.R.R. Kingfisher?*"

"*Pah! Before he pilfered me from my previous owners, he was but a pimply ignoramus known as* Gilbert.*"* The quill spat the name like a curse. *"It was I who molded and shaped him into the novelist and the moniker he was lucky enough to die with! Now,"* the quill continued, humming with fervor, *"you must take me to your place of domicile. There, you will arrange for me a large pile of unblemished parchment and an endless pot of ink from which I may dip my nib to create the most beautiful, heart-rending story ever told – my own!"*

"Hang on a minute," Chet said slowly. "Do you mean to tell me that *you* were the one who wrote all those stories? Not the authors, but…you?"

The quill abruptly stilled.

Chet let out a soft gasp, his eyes narrowing at the quill he was clutching like a dagger. "You were the one who wrote G.R.R. Kingfisher's 'Falston Records'? *You're* the reason he became a multi-national bestselling urban fantasy author?"

"Er…"

"This changes everything," Chet whispered, avarice glinting in his beady little eyes. *"Everything."*

"Oh, no." The stiffened plume of the quill abruptly drooped, then hung limply. *"You're a..."* It gulped, then tried again. *"A writer?"*

"Not just any writer!" Chet bit his lip. "Soon, I'll be known as the greatest, most brilliant writer that ever lived!"

"How?" the quill lamented. *"How do they always manage to find me...?"* He gazed up at Chet, quivering. *"Please, sir, bestow mercy upon me and hurl me into the swamps so that I may fester in peace!"*

But Chet had long stopped listening. He was already revving the engine, his racing mind adrift in all the deliciously vicious ways he would rub his newfound success in his brother's pitiful, sniveling face.

Back in the cramped solitude of his one-bedroom apartment, Chet ungallantly tossed an armful of overflowing boxes to the ground, crossed the living room – ignoring the broken mug and coffee stains – and cleared off his desk with one exuberant swipe of the arm that sent his computer monitor, piles of notebooks, chewed-on pencil nubs, and worn-out thesaurus scattering across the floor. Then, with a knight-like flourish, he withdrew the quill from his back pocket, yanked some paper out of the printer tray, and sat down to write.

Except he had no ink.

Chet tapped the nib against his lip

thoughtfully, oblivious to the quill's frantic attempts to squirm free. "Now where can I get my hands on some ink…?" His eyes darted to a pale blue vein running along his forearm. "I could pen it in my own blood, a testament to my staggering genius and sacrifice laid bare upon the paper." He crinkled his nose. "Of course, having a finite amount of blood, it would be difficult to properly pen my masterwork without leeching myself dry in the process—"

"How poetic." The quill sighed in spite of himself.

"Hard to make money when you're dead, though." Chet's eyes settled on the hall closet. "Aha! Brilliant!" He rose from the desk, yanked open the closet door and rummaged around the pile of footwear sitting at the bottom until he rose triumphantly, black shoe polish in hand.

"Oh, for the love of the Creator!" the quill moaned. *"You can't—"* His protests ended in a gurgle as Chet dunked him into the tub of glop.

"Okay," Chet mused, holding the squirrelly quill above the once-blank sheet, now splattered in flecks of shoe polish: the promise of forthcoming brilliance. "I *could* take another stab at

'*The Magician's Apprentice's Daughter*'—"

The quill, which was still coughing and sputtering on the gloppy shoe polish, let out a woeful moan. "*Creator, spare me. Please!*"

"—but why mess with perfection?" Chet tapped the quill thoughtfully, further besmirching the paper. "No. I need something else. Something new." His eyebrows climbed his forehead, and his eyes brightened. "I've got it!"

If a quill could facepalm, this one would be doing exactly that.

"I've been thinking about this story for ages but was never quite sure how to package it." Chet stroked his chin, smearing it with shoe polish in the process. "Basically, it should start with Chert Bingham, the world-renowned detective-slash-acclaimed-astrophysicist and his buxom blonde paramour, Charlize, who he's just rescued from the gaping maw of a kraken-like alien that's invaded earth for our water, which is extremely rare and valuable on the aliens' home world because all of theirs evaporated from a large asteroid impact... Did you get all that?"

The quill gaped at him in horror. *"Do you write as poorly as you speak? Please, death would be preferable to this!"*

Chet impatiently tapped its nib on the paper. "Write!"

"Shakespeare forgive me," the quill sighed. Then, with a resigned sigh, it began to hum. A warm glow spread through the metal shaft, illuminating the strange symbols that had been etched along its length.

And then the quill began to write.

Ichor and bile spewed from the disembodied tentacles of the gargantuan extraterrestrial invader, brackish and bilious and black as the night sky from whence it hailed. Like a babe cutting himself free from the confines of his placenta, Chert Bingham emerged from the hewn bowels of the felled beast, his hard-earned muscles glinting with perspiration and the mawkish gore of this unwelcome interstellar abomination.

"Hey...that's not half-bad!" Chet mused, holding up the page. "But what about Charlize? And can you make sure to add something about her heaving bosoms? Also, don't forget to make Chert extra heroic. Like Dwayne Johnson."

"*I thought you imagined yourself an author of fantasy?*" the quill grumbled. "*Aliens from the very depths of the wide oceans are* not *from the realms of fantasy.*"

"It's urban fantasy." Chet smiled. "Anything goes!"

The quill heaved a long suffering sigh.

Silence descended upon the gore-saturated battleground, a blackened and scorched stretch of earth where life would return one day, and such life would owe its continued existence to Chert Bingham.

"Chert?" a musical voice called — the voice of a woman who required reassurance. Strength. Wisdom. Chert possessed all three. "Is it over? Are we safe?"

Chert's stony gaze fell on the

shadows invading the collapsed buildings that had been left in the monstrous beast's ruinous wake. From within the smothering darkness, its tendrils swirling with pregnant malice, Charlize emerged, a lone sparkling star amidst the darkest skies. Tears stained her porcelain face as she fell into Chert's liberating embrace.

He ran his thumb across her cheek. "I wish I could tell you it was, my darling. Alas, the battle for Earth is far from over."

A soft whimper escaped her throat. As her prodigious bosoms heaved with a sob, her close-fitting battle armor—

"No, not battle-armor," Chet interjected. "A dress!"

"*A dress?*" the quill sputtered. "*But they have been doing battle with a kraken-like alien! Why in all the pages of the world would Charlize wear a* dress?!"

"Because it's *my* story. You're just my ghost writer." Chet tapped the page with an insistent forefinger. "Make it a dress. A short one. With lots of rips in it."

"*Unbearable!*" the quill wailed. "*The lot of you insufferable writers! Fine, if this story must be written, then it shall be written to a higher standard than it deserves!*"

"And make her barefoot." Chet licked his lips. "My readers will love that."

"*Ugh,*" the quill moaned. It scratched out the last of its words, and continued on.

> *Dress torn to ribbons, and her once-perfectly manicured toes dirtied by the gore still oozing from the conquered creature, Charlize glanced demurely away from Chert's open study. Her chest heaved as she stood before him, straight of back, her ripe breasts straining against the—*

"*Must I really write this?*" the quill asked, feather trembling. "This is like George R.R. Martin all over again!"

"Yes!" Chet snapped. "You have to do exactly—wait a minute. You wrote for George R.R. Martin?"

"Indeed." The quill sniffed. "*Before I fell into G.R.R. Kingfisher's possession over a decade ago, a pair of writers shared me: George R.R. Martin and Patrick Rothfuss.*" It shivered. "*But they began squabbling over me with increasing belligerence. One night, as Patrick and George wrestled on the floor of the former's study, G.R.R. climbed through the open window and purloined me from the drawer in which I had been safely cradled. Clearly my legend had spread amongst you...writers. Their howls of agony echoed through the night as G.R.R. absconded with me into the safety of the growing shadows.*"

"Wow." Chet leaned back in his chair. "Well, at least with me you'll get to finish our manuscripts."

The quill's feather wilted like a daisy. "*Yes.*" It sighed. "*I suppose there is that. A small mercy to a helpless, magical quill created by Cadmus, the Greek god of writing. If only he could see my tortured fate. Perhaps then he never would have—"*

"Can we get a move on with the story?" Chet interjected. "You were about to describe her straining breasts."

Flashing Chet a filthy look he could not see, the quill continued.

—her ripe breasts straining against the tattered remains of her skin-tight silk dress. "You're my hero, Chert," she whispered, taking a small step toward him with arched bare feet, her fingers finding the chiseled musculature of his forearm. Her cheeks bloomed with cherry-tinted diffidence. "You're everyone's hero."

Chert pulled Charlize closer and pressed his lips to hers, savoring her sweet taste. "Don't call me a hero," he growled.

She trembled, like his robust masculinity fed her the energy to live. To go on. She pressed her fingers against her parted lips as if she could contain the sensation of his mouth.

As dawn broke over the desolation of broken buildings and smoking wreckage, Chert's chest rose and fell in a deep, steeling breath. Indeed, the battle was far from over. Chert Bingham had long been a world-renowned detective-slash-acclaimed-astrophysicist; but right then, he was also Earth's best bet for survival.

And there was no better bet than Chert Bingham.

The quill came to a stop and sighed. "*Is that what you are looking for? What you demand from me? This...pulp!*"

Chet blew on the glistening pages, admiring the perfect cursive. A broad, toothy smile spread across his face. "Yes. This is *exactly* what I want. Tasteful Harem Urban Fantasy, written by the masterful C.R.R.R.T.J. Williams, and it's going to make me a millionaire!"

"'C.R.R.R.T.J.' Williams?" the quill repeated. "*Is that not too many initials?*"

"No, it's just enough! Now, let's get to work. I've got so many plans! Once we've finished this book, I've got another brilliant idea for a story about a warrior-turned-farmer named Chett of Mallia who's summoned to rescue a dozen princesses stolen by an evil wizard named Jonn. It's been rattling around in my brain for *years*."

The quill's feather shook, then sagged. *"And then?"*

"After that, we'll begin the erotic western steampunk saga featuring Chetre de Williamsberg, the Michelin-star chef-slash-retired spy who—"

"After your seemingly unremitting ideas are penned," the quill interjected. *"Will you do one courtesy for me? Just one, measly act of kindness?"*

Chet's eyes narrowed. "And what's that?"

"Will you help me attain my first and singular wish of penning an original tale...one published under my own *name?"*

"Your magnus opum, huh?"

"Yes, *my*..." the quill shook. *"Magnus opum?! It is 'magnum opus'!"*

"Opum, opus, whatever." Chet considered the quill's request, then shrugged. "Why not?"

"*Very well*," the quill whispered, working to contain its trembling excitement. *"At least this is better than being left forgotten and bereft at the bottom of a box, crushed by meaningless bric-a-brac for decades."* Its feather swirled with an invigorated flourish. *"Let us create, C.R.R.R.T.J. Williams. Let us create."*

Four

A full year had passed since Chet's fortuitous discovery of G.R.R. Kingfisher's magic quill. Since then, the expensive, unending supply of paper and ink had more than paid for itself; in the span of three hundred and sixty-five days and three hundred and sixty-five nights, the quill had penned eleven full-length novels, nine novelettes, twenty-three short stories, and a collection of "intimate poetry" that Chet had commissioned to showcase his "impressive repertoire of bedroom excursions." At first, Chet lurked directly above the quill as it toiled, salivating like a bear freshly woken from hibernation as he read each nascent word.

But over time, Chet grew more and more bored with the endeavor. Soon, detailed read-throughs turned to cursory edits; not long after, cursory edits became casual glances. Eventually, Chet abandoned the effort altogether, granting – through sheer apathy – the quill complete control over "their" masterpieces while he planted himself in front of his PlayStation.

Not-so-coincidentally, critical reception of C.R.R.R.T.J. Williams' prodigious and ever-growing collection of works grew ever more positive. But it was Chet's – or rather, the quill's – most recent manuscript, *The Heartbreak of Triumph,* which changed everything. For all Chet knew, the book chronicled the valiant adventures of the well-hung huntsman, Will Chettams, his doting and curvaceous valet, Genevieve, and his arch-nemesis, the gnome-giant, Jon al'Smallwillie. In actuality, the quill had secretly penned a poignant and heart-wrenching tale about an impoverished bread maker, his cancer-stricken yet ever faithful hound dog, and the relentless struggle of finding joy in the depths of soul-crushing sorrow.

The book was an overnight success. *The*

Heartbreak of Triumph soared to the top of the New York Times Bestseller list, rocketing Chet to instant fame. Within weeks, Chet's face was plastered on the cover of every literary magazine and on the front of every bookstore window. He'd been booked for signings, convention appearances, and primetime news segments. Several book-to-film adaptations were in the works, and Netflix had been reaching out every other day for a month about some streaming special they'd been wanting to do. Numerous editors from the 'Big Five' had been hassling him to buy his backlist and inquiring about any other completed works he had tucked away in his desk. They'd even shown interest in *The Magician's Apprentice's Daughter*, and they all said they *loved* the title.

Chet had never been so busy, or so miserable, in his entire life. He was living his greatest dream – the life of a world-renowned celebrity fiction writer – thanks to a book he had nothing to do with.

As he trudged through the massive New York City bookstore to take his seat at his fourth book signing for the week, he shot the long line of readers waiting for him an assortment of filthy looks. The moment he slumped into his uncomfortable folding chair, a mousy, middle-aged woman with thick glasses approached him, reverently clutching *The Heartbreak of Triumph* against her chest.

"It is such an honor to meet you, Mr. Williams," she enthused, blinking back tears.

"Call me C.R.R.R.T.J.," he muttered, holding out an expectant hand.

She handed him the book with two trembling hands. "The way you described the bone-deep excavation that loss carves into one's being, and how, without that 'crucible of agony,' as you so aptly put it, we would have nothing in which to pour the 'molten grandeur' of joy…" she trailed off, wiping the tears in her eyes.

"Uh huh." Chet scribbled something illegible inside the cover.

"O, if I were but little happy, if I could say how much!" a muffled voice trilled from inside his messenger bag.

Chet kicked it.

"What was that?" the woman asked,

dabbing an eye with her handkerchief. When Chet didn't reply, she blew her nose loudly, then added, "I just…I've never read anything that resonated so deeply in my spirit—"

"Next!" the author barked, thrusting the book back in her hands.

"But I—"

"Next!!"

The woman slunk off, paving the way for the next person in line – a lanky teenager with pockmarked skin and intensive orthodontia. "Mr. Williams—"

"It's C.R.R.T.J.," Chet sniped, snatching the book from the boy's hands. "Who do I make it out to?"

"To Timothy—"

"For Tim," Chet muttered, scrawling the letters with a violent flourish.

"Actually, I'd prefer—"

"For. *Tim*." Chet glared at him as he violently dotted the *i*. "Next!"

It continued like this for an unreasonably torturous forty-five minutes – with readers doting, quills lamenting, and cramping hands inscribing – until a familiar voice murmured,

"Hello, Chet."

Chet's head snapped up so quickly his C4 vertebra let out a loud *pop!* "J-Jon!" he stammered, leaping to his feet. "You came?"

His younger brother smiled down at him with perfect, pearly teeth. "Of course I came! How could I not support my only brother in what has been the success of a lifetime!" he scooped Chet into a tight hug that squeezed the air from his lungs. "I read every word of this masterpiece!" he enthused, tapping the front cover of *The Heartbreak of Triumph.* "Honestly, Chet, I didn't think you had it in you – especially after you sent me that literary travesty earlier last year. What a mess that was!"

A shooting pain zinged through Chet's grinding jaw.

"I mean, the way you used the forming and kneading of bread to epitomize the struggle of man! And the synecdochic allegory of yeast to represent the fermentation and upheaval of stolen youth! Clearly, you should have left fantasy behind a long time ago!"

"What's wrong with fantasy?" Chet growled, squeezing the life out of his Sharpie.

"Nothing!" A wide, gleaming smile spread across Jon's face. "But *The Heartbreak of Triumph* transcends genre. The way you brought Greek tragedy into it while keeping it relevant to the bread maker's plight. Remarkable!"

The quill let out a loud sniffle. *"At last! A true afficionado of genius!"*

"What was that?" Jon asked.

"I said, 'Glad you finally appreciate my genius," Chet answered, giving his messenger bag a swift kick. "What with the yeast and the bread and all those Greeks."

"Yes…" Jon frowned. "Anyway, after reading the book – no less than three times cover to cover, I admit – what I really wanted to ask you…" He ran a self-conscious hand through his obnoxiously perfect coif of hair. "Regarding the line Malachi utters just before succumbing to the fatal wounds he sustained from the wheat grinder he was finally able to afford after selling all those loaves of bread to pay for his dog's cancer treatments—"

Chet shifted uncomfortably.

"What exactly did Malachi mean when he

uttered, 'I shall ferry the rolling tide of eternal sleep across the threshold as my bride'? Was that in reference to embracing the inexorability of mortality, or rather the lassitude of enduring that which is required to remain ephemeral, i.e., ardor and verve?"

Chet stared at him blankly. "Um…the second one."

Something inside his messenger bag thumped loudly.

The line between Jon's brows deepened. "But if that's the case, then why—"

"Next!" Chet screeched, then forced an amiable-sounding chuckle through gritted teeth. "Sorry, brother, but if I talk to you all day, then I won't be able to chat with all of my other doting fans who have been waiting so patiently for my autograph! I think I see a few fantasy fans, and you know what they're like. Yak, yak, yak." He laughed a little too loudly as he scrawled something on the inside cover of his brother's book. "Anyway, it was great seeing you! We'll chat again soon. *Next!*"

"Chet?"

He looked up at his younger brother. The

wide grin had evaporated from Jon's face and his eyes were alit with suspicion.

Chet swallowed. "What?"

"You've got that look on your face."

"What look?"

Jon lowered his voice to a conspiratorial murmur. "Like when we were left in that motel room as kids and you spent a fortune on those…*ahem*…spicy channels. And then claimed you knew nothing about it when Mom and Dad got the four-hundred-dollar bill from Pay-Per-View…"

Chet's giggle rose to a pitch that only dogs and dolphins could hear. "I don't know what you're talking about."

"I've read all of your stuff, you know? Even though you thought I didn't. I did." Jon hefted a copy of *The Heartbreak of Triumph*. "Something changed after that *Magician's Apprentice's Daughter* trainwreck. It all changed there."

The bag twitched. Chet put his foot on it, muffling the quill before it could cry out.

He swallowed, unable to meet his brother's glare. "Practice makes perfect."

Jon's eyes had narrowed to thin slits. "Chet, say it isn't so."

"Say what isn't so?"

Chet recoiled as Jon pressed both hands on the table, then leaned in so close their noses were almost touching. "You aren't using a...a..." He cleared his throat, then lowered his voice even further, as though uttering a racial epithet. "...a *ghostwriter*, are you?"

"Who, me?" Chet squeaked, his eyes darting to his messenger bag.

"You *are*." Jon's hiss slithered. "You're paying someone to write for you, aren't you? Giving them a quick buck and then putting your name on their work?"

"Shh!" Chet tried to hush him. "I didn't—"

"I am not even being compensated for my genius!" The quill's strangled cry tore out of the messenger bag.

"All these people." Jon thrust his finger at the line of impatient onlookers, then jabbed it back in Chet's face. "All these people have paid their hard-earned money to read *your* books. They buy *your* merchandise. They come into the city and line up for *hours* so you can scrawl

C.R.R.T Will —"

"C.R.R.*R*.T.*J*. Williams," Chet growled, leaning over to snatch his messenger bag. The fans nearest him and his brother exchanged wide-eyed, indignant glances.

"Did you hear that?" one of them loudly muttered to the other. "This guy's a fraud!"

"Your fans deserve the truth, Chet." Jon slammed *The Heartbreak of Triumph* on the table between them, the thud's echo spreading like the harbinger of doom. *Chet's* doom. A tight silence followed; all eyes turned their way. All ears, too. "*Who* is writing your books?!"

"Not 'who,' but 'what,' as 'who' can only refer to—"

Chet gave his messenger bag a hard swat. "Gotta go!" he cried, launching to his feet, messenger bag pressed to his chest, the quill's muffled cries were swallowed by shouts of rage from the line of angry bookworms.

He ran around the table, eyes fixed on the all-too-far away exit. While Chet's characters might have boasted the dexterity and athleticism of Olympic gymnasts, Chet sadly did not. His feet caught in the tangle of his ungainly legs, and his ungainly legs slammed into the plant pot that had been inconveniently stationed beside his signing table.

The plant pot crashed onto its side, soil spilling from it like a surge of ants. Chet dove forward, feet scrambling for purchase on the treacherously well-polished floor, his messenger bag flying out of his hands in slow motion. A wordless cry tore from Chet's throat as gravity and rotten circumstance freed the trapped contents. The hapless author hit the deck, bouncing from the impact as air rushed from his lungs.

"It is I!" crowed the quill, its feather quivering whilst it lay on the bookstore's gleaming floor as Chet's scrambling fingers reached for it. *"I am the genius behind all of Chet's work. And Shakespeare's and Homer's and Orwell's and Vonnegut's! And* The Heartbreak of Triumph *is mine!* My *magnum opus! The work my feather and nib have desired to etch on glorious blank sheets since—"*

Chet grabbed the object of his torment the same way he'd long desired to throttle Jon's neck. The quill's triumphant proclamations ended in an indignant squawk as Chet shoved it into his back pocket and sprinted for the exit.

Cries followed him. Of confusion. Of panic. Of obscenities. Even an alarm rang out, but that could quite easily have been Chet's imagination. Abandoning his belongings, Chet plowed through the crowds of people who were deliberately blocking his path to freedom. Hands jostled him. Sneering mouths opened and words spilled out, but he heard nothing. Only the exit to the New York City sidewalk mattered. Nothing else.

He burst out of the store and doubled over, panting like he'd run the city marathon. The doors behind him banged open, and pure self-preservation alone propelled him into movement.

"Cab! I need a cab!" he gasped, sprinting down the sidewalk. Waves of New York noise slammed into him as he bolted. Horns. Bellows. Engines revving. Alarms blaring.

"Someone get me a goddamn cab!" he screamed into the sky, and divine intervention lent a helping hand.

A dirty yellow vehicle pulled over, its

window already wound down, the gum-chewing, grizzled cab driver staring expectantly. Chet dove into the back seat and slammed the door behind him.

"JFK Airport!" he pleaded, hands pressed against his chest, his hammering heart pushing against his palms. "I've got to get home. Home!"

"Sure thing, buddy. Might wanna fasten your seatbelt."

Before Chet could fasten any such thing, the driver hit the gas, sending Chet's forehead crashing into the back of the seat, then slammed on the brakes, propelling him backwards again. This continued for several minutes as the cab jerked by the bookstore, where Jon and a large crowd of people had gathered outside the doors. Chet turned away.

They all know. I'm ruined. Finished! And once the rest of them find out... Chet breathed in slowly through his nose then exhaled just as slowly, a smile spreading across his lips. *Find out what? That a* magical quill *wrote my books?! Who would believe them? Hell, the rest of the world will chalk it up to a jealous younger brother.* He snorted. *Sure, Jon – a magical quill!*

Chet sniggered, and leaned back into the seat, rolling his shoulders. "You're awfully quiet after your little performance," he whisper-hissed over his shoulder. "You and I are gonna have a little talk when we get home, just you wait."

The quill, for once, stayed silent.

"What?" Chet prodded. "Got nothing to say for yourself?"

Not a single sound rose from the quill. Not even the slightest twitch of its feather tickled Chet's backside.

Scowling, he twisted in his seat and stuck his hand into his back pocket... And grasped nothing but lint.

"No!" Chet whispered. He patted his rear, then his other pockets. His jacket.

Nothing.

"NO!" he howled, turning to look out of the cab's rear window, his sweaty palms pressing against the glass. He'd lost the quill! But where? In the store? On the sidewalk? He couldn't go back, not with Jon waiting, not with all his fans clamoring for an explanation.

"Crap!" Tears stung his eyes and each labored breath burned.

"Everything alright, buddy?" the cab driver called, frowning into his rear-view.

"I'm ruined," Chet shouted, pulling at his hair. *"Ruined!"*

"Well, that's New York," the cab driver shrugged. "Happens to everyone once or twice." He turned up the radio and fixed his eyes on the road.

Chet hid his face in his hands, only the seat belt's resistance keeping him upright.

"What am I going to do now?" he sobbed into his palms.

But no one answered.

Miserable, tired, and ravenously hungry, Chet stumbled into his apartment and chucked his key on the kitchen countertop. His cell phone had died somewhere above North Carolina, and he'd left his charger in his messenger bag. Back in the bookstore.

Back with the quill.

Chet dropped his forehead to the countertop, thumping it against the cool Formica. That stupid quill couldn't have been the only magical quill out there. He'd just have to scour the internet for another one. A *better* one.

Except... Chet's head shot up. What if it really *was* one of a kind? *Then what?*

He shook his throbbing head roughly. He had enough money and royalties coming in to live off. He had time on his side. Time enough to make some blog posts about an 'unfortunate family issue' at his latest signing in New York, and he needed to take a little break from the road and social media, but did anyone happen to locate the possessions he'd left behind? Including a silly-old quill? Worthless, really, but it had sentimental value. That's all.

No. The quill would talk. The quill *always* talked.

Chet dropped into his chair in front of his monitor and fired it up. He'd have to retire. Live on the royalties of his work.

The *quill's* work.

"Maybe all I need is a new pen name. C.H. Williams." He rubbed at his chin. "It has a ring to it... Well, maybe one more letter for stylistic oomph."

After his computer loaded, he scanned his various social media networks, expecting a barrage of accusations of plagiarism. Twitter yielded nothing but the usual praise about his unrivaled genius and queries about what he planned to do next. Instagram posts tagged him in artfully taken photos of his book covers, and TikTok showed nothing but excited BookTokers reviewing his latest work and spreading their praise to whoever would sit through their fifteen-seconds of piggy-backed fame.

"Alright…" Chet murmured, switching to his email, his shoulders relaxing for the first time since fleeing New York. "I can live with this."

Signing requests filled his inbox. Royalty statements. Interview requests. Chet's eyes widened, his cursor hovering over an email with the title: 'THE MAGICIAN'S APPRENTICE'S DAUGHTER' from an editor at one of the Big Five publishers. Breath trapped in his chest, Chet clicked on it.

"Dear Mr. Williams, I hope this email finds you well. Thank you for your swift reply regarding *The Magician's Apprentice's Daughter*, and for providing me with a copy of the manuscript. It was most illuminating. While it is…different…than your latest oeuvre, and a little rougher around the edges than I was expecting, I believe there is a need to strike while the iron is hot. While *The Magician's Apprentice's Daughter* is not to *my* taste, that is not to say your millions of fans would not enjoy it. We have made you a generous offer (see attachment one) for the manuscript, and for a sequel. Our thinking is to release them side-by-side in order to exploit the explosion in your popularity and the interest in your work. Book one will need expanding, of course, and I have provided notes (see attachment two) but we can discuss those another time. If another publisher offers you similar, we will outbid them. Mr. Williams, this is your time, and I will be your erstwhile champion, just like Chête, a character soon to beloved in the world of fantasy, I have no doubt."

Chet read the email a second time. Then a third.

An offer. For his own work. One the quill had nothing to do with. Nothing! He drummed his fingers on the table and smiled.

"Well, if *The Heartbreak of Triumph* is the quill's 'magnus opum,' *The Magician's Apprentice's Daughter's Younger Sister* will be mine. And it'll be even more magnus than the quill's. You can bet the farm on that!"

Chet typed out a hasty reply, e-signing the agreement but not bothering to look at the fine print or attachments, then minimized the window – only to immediately reopen it. Right there, at the top of his email provider, was the bold, red font of a Breaking News alert: "BESTSELLING AUTHOR TEAMS UP WITH MAGICAL QUILL IN GROUNDBREAKING LITERARY COLLABORATION." Chet hesitated, then clicked on the link, black feathering his vision and blood roaring in his ears. A video popped up on the screen, featuring his brother standing next to a beautiful mixed-race news anchor. Chet couldn't help but wonder which part of the Orient she was from.

"I'm standing here with Jon A. Williams," the buxom reporter started, holding the microphone up to her plump mouth, *"the three-time-Hugo-Award-Winning, number-one New York Times Bestselling author, who has just announced a literary partnership so astonishing, you might think it came straight from one of his universally-critically-*

acclaimed, multi-award-winning fantasy books. But that only goes to show that real life truly is stranger than fiction, isn't that right, Jon?"

His younger brother let out a wry chuckle that made Chet's fingernails dig into the wood of his writing desk. *"Yes, Mei, that certainly does seem to be the case. But please don't take my word for it."* He opened up his suit jacket, withdrawing something from the inner pocket that made Chet's throat close so tightly, he gave up on breathing altogether. *"Mei, I'd like you to meet my very close friend, Quilliam."*

The news anchor and Chet let out simultaneous gasps as Jon held up a black ostrich feather quill to the microphone…a black ostrich feather quill that began to speak for all the world to hear.

"A copacetic diurnal course to you, Mei, whose beauty is like a rich jewel in an Ethiope's ear; Beauty too rich for use, for earth too dear!"

"Oh, you flatter me, Quilliam!" the strumpet laughed, clearly eating up every word.

Now that I look at her, Chet seethed, *she could stand to lose a few pounds.*

"*Please, my sweet lotus blossom, call me Quill!*"

"*So, Quill*"—she stroked his feather flirtatiously—"*tell me, is it true you had been enslaved for centuries—*"

"*Millennia,*" Jon interjected, his expression somber.

"*—for millennia,*" she clicked her tongue, "*before Mr. Williams freed you from your servitude?*"

The quill's feather drooped. "*Indeed. Since my inception, I have been used – and abused – as a mere writing instrument for those far less talented vagabonds who robbed me of my words and published them as their own.*"

Chet was grinding his teeth so hard, pain zinged through both sides of his jaw.

"*Please accept my deepest condolences for the hardships you've endured,*" Mei cooed, twirling his feather between her slender fingers. "*Speaking of which, do you have any comments about the rumors that C.R.R.R.T.J. Williams was one of the authors who imprisoned you, claiming your work as his own?*"

"*We have no comment about that,*" Jon

interjected hastily, *"save to express our fervent wish that Chet receive the help and support he so desperately needs during what is sure to be a very difficult time for him."*

Chet's back molar cracked from the pressure of his jaw. "Ow!" he yelped, clapping his hand against the right side of his face.

"What Quilliam and I would much prefer to talk about," Jon continued, *"is our upcoming project,* The Tragedy of Victory, *which is loosely based on Quilliam's harrowing experiences as a maltreated magical muse through the centuries. Though I have offered my humble services and world-renowned editing and publishing team, Quilliam himself will be taking the lead on the story, penning it under his own name for the first time in centuries—"*

"Millennia," the quill interjected.

"Millennia," Jon amended somberly. *"The positive news being, of course, that we were offered the largest advance payment in publishing history, the majority of which will go toward funding writing programs in underprivileged schools, of course. And, as you've probably seen in the headlines, we've already*

shattered pre-order records, with over 250 million copies sold before even entering the first draft stage—"

Chet's computer monitor flew across the room, smashing against the wall, sending plastic and plaster raining down on the coffee-stained carpeting. "I'll show them...I'll show them *both*," he seethed, his shoulders rising and falling in poorly contained fury.

With that, he got to work.

After hauling his old typewriter out of his bedroom closet, he muted all notifications on his phone, disabled his social media accounts, drew the blinds, and set the away message on his emails. He then unplugged his television and packed away his beloved PlayStation, arranged for his groceries and toiletries to be delivered, and tacked a sign on the outside of his front door that read, "SILENCE – ACCLAIMED WRITER AT WORK!" His only companion was the framed photo of G.R.R. Kingfisher he'd stolen from his late hero's home office, which gazed up at him from beside the keyboard in proud reverence.

The silence initially took some getting used to, so Chet cranked Vivaldi up to full volume, drowning out the intrusive thoughts of self-doubt, the sounds of his neighbor's broom banging on the ceiling, the unflinching disappointment in Jon's voice when he'd discovered Chet had been using a ghost writer in the form of a magical quill.

Chet ground his teeth, his fingers picking up speed. Though the muscles in his wrist had long ago atrophied, he pushed through the cramping discomfort with a family-sized bottle of acetaminophen. In this elevated state of mental capacity, this higher realm of creativity and beauty, pain scarcely registered. Hunger meant nothing. Fatigue, merely an obstacle to rise above.

Meals were forgotten, sleep abandoned.

And yet, words poured from Chet's calloused fingers, lyrical and heartfelt and raw. In truth, he'd never worked so hard, so feverishly, so wholeheartedly and unreservedly in his life. For years, Chet finally understood, he'd subconsciously held himself back, too afraid that his best effort would result in failure, that he would wither away in his brother's shadow. But now, there was no room for fear, nor for ego. The only thing that mattered was Chet's magnum opus: His future. His redemption. His salvation.

Weeks passed, though, for Chet, the passage of time no longer registered. Summer turned to Fall, Fall to Winter, and Winter to Spring.

Finally, just as the pale blossoms of late spring were budding into the lush greenery of early summer, an astonished gasp slipped from Chet's mouth. For the first time in months, his fingers halted their possessed flurry, poising over the keyboard in trembling suspension. Eyes transfixed to the page, Chet slowly typed out the final two words of his two-hundred-thousand word masterpiece, a deep, shuddering sob slipping through his lips as the carriage of the typewriter returned for the final time.

"I did it," he rasped, staggering to his feet as he tore the final page from his typewriter, the last of six-hundred pages that he had poured his blood, sweat, and tears into. His hand shook as he brought the page to his face, still warm, the fresh ink glistening. "I never needed a magic quill to be great." A fresh sob shuddered through him as he clutched the page against his heart. "Greatness was here, in me, all along."

He reverently set the final page upon the meticulously stacked manuscript resting on his desk, then strode across the living room and flung open the blinds, bathing his apartment in golden, honied light for the first time in nearly a year. He cranked open his window, welcoming his first breath of fresh air into his neglected lungs…then froze.

Arms crossed in front of his unfairly muscular chest, with his stolen magical quill in hand, Jon stared down at Chet from the billboard across the street – the one that used to advertise Del Taco's breakfast burritos – his pearly-white teeth practically glowing in the sunlight. Beside his towering image was the award-emblazoned front cover of *The Tragedy of Victory*, alongside the words, "1.6 BILLION COPIES SOLD!"

"No." Chet backed away from the window, his hand clapped over his mouth in horror. His foot landed in the wastebasket, which sent him sprawling backward, his arms flailing like a windmill. As he crashed head-first into his desk, all 600 pages of *The Magician's Apprentice's*

Daughter's Younger Sister went scattering across the room, with the final page fluttering atop Chet's unconscious face.

Two hours later, as Chet was being carted into the ambulance by three EMT's who were plugging their noses at his eye-watering body odor, the firefighter who'd broken down Chet's front door reached down to snatch the piece of paper from the ground, crinkling his nose in distaste as he read it. "You've gotta be kidding me."

A second firefighter looked up from the hazmat sign he was busy tacking to Chet's front door. "What now?"

"Get a load of this!" the first snorted, reading aloud from the page. "Chête threw his head back and roared out a booming, manly laugh, so manly it made Jonn cower like a frightened woman. That skinny, talentless wizard cried right there on the spot, knowing he had been bested by the *far* better wizard. The far better *man*. 'Oh, Chête!' Angelina cried, her eyes big and breasts even bigger as they jiggled with excitement. 'Take me here and now. I do not care who is watching, so long as you ravish me like Jonn never could!' Chête's laugh was rich and masculine. 'Come here, my sweet!' Chête boomed at the wizard's apprentice's daughter's younger sister, his eyes surveying the rest of the scantily dressed harem he had rescued from Jonn's fungus-ridden claws. 'And the brunette and redhead, too! I will ravish you all in a way Jonn never could!' All twelve of the women ran at him, their enormous breasts bouncing with anticipation…'" The firefighter let out a low whistle. "It just goes on and on like this."

"Jesus." His colleague shook his head in disbelief. "My dog could write a better story than that."

"No kidding." The first firefighter crumpled the page into a ball and tossed it in the wastebasket with the rest of the trash he'd gathered from the floor. "Speaking of which, have you read Jon A. Williams' new book yet? My wife says it's fantastic."

About the Authors

RACHEL RENER is an award-winning, #1 international bestselling urban fantasy author who loves blurring the line between science and magic. She graduated from the University of Colorado after focusing on Psychology and Neuroscience. Since then, she has lived on three continents and has traveled to more than 40 countries.

When she's not engrossed in writing or reading, Rachel enjoys art of all kinds, riding her motorcycle, going to rock shows (both musical and mineralogical), Vulcanology (the lava kind as well as the pointy-eared variety), and being the voice behind Tana the Tiefling on the popular DnD podcast, *Of Dice and Friends*.

She lives in Colorado along with her husband and a feisty umbrella cockatoo named Terrance (a.k.a "Jungle Chicken") that hangs out on her shoulder as she writes – whether invited or not.

Learn more at www.RachelRener.com.

Other Works by Rachel Rener:

The Gilded Blood Series
I. Inked
II. Jinxed
III. Linked
IV. Synced
The Gilded Blood Limited Edition Omnibus

The Lightning Conjurer Series
I. The Awakening
II. The Enlightening
III. The Christening
IV. The Reckoning
The Complete Series Collection

The Bone Whisperer Chronicles
I. The Girl Who Talks to Ashes
II. The Boy Who Lurks in Shadows

The Little Morsel

The Precipice of Sin
(As part of the *From the Shadows* Anthology)

Autographed Books Available at
~ www.RachelRener.com ~

About the Authors

DAVID GREEN is a neurodivergent writer of the epic and the urban, the fantastical and the mysterious.

With his character-driven dark fantasy series Empire Of Ruin, or urban fantasy noir HELL IN HAVEN, David takes readers on emotional, action-packed thrill rides.

Hailing from the north-west of England, David now lives in County Galway on the west coast of Ireland with his wife and train-obsessed son.

When not writing, David can be found wondering why he chooses to live in places where it constantly rains.

David's Path Of War was nominated for the Robert Holdstock Best Fantasy Novel at the British Fantasy Awards 2023.

Learn more at linktr.ee/davidgreenwriter

OTHER WORKS BY DAVID GREEN

THE 'EMPIRE OF RUIN' SERIES
0. Before The Shadow
I. In Solitude's Shadow
II. Path Of War
III. Beyond Sundered Seas
IV. At Eternity's Gates

THE 'HELL IN HAVEN' SERIES
0. Nick Holleran vs Whiskey Pete's
I. The Devil Walks In Blood Special Edition
II. One Life Left

NOTABLE ANTHOLOGIES
With Blood And Ash
Sky Breaker: Tales of the Wanderer

Printed in Great Britain
by Amazon

8b9f428c-7ca3-4cb8-a811-e93bef3557acR01